MOON and STAR

A Christmas Story

Robin Muller

North Winds Press
An imprint of Scholastic Canada Ltd.

Jacket photo: Chip Jones

Library and Archives Canada Cataloguing in Publication
Muller, Robin
Moon and Star / Robin Muller.
ISBN 0-439-97466-6
I. Title.
PS8576.U424M66 2005   jC813'.54   C2005-901032-0

6 5 4 3 2 1   Printed in Canada   05 06 07 08

To Samantha Youssef,
the angel at the top of the
Christmas tree

and to
Chip Jones,
a dear friend and
patient adviser.

Long ago, in a shop filled with toys, there lived a dog. He was large and gentle, with a moon-shaped mark around his eye. The old lady who owned the shop called him Moon.

Moon loved all the toys, but secretly he loved one above all the others: a delicate little porcelain cat with a shining star painted on its face. Moon called the cat Star, and he wanted her to be his alone. Every night, after the old lady had gone to bed, Moon would carry Star to his mat by the stove. There he would curl himself around her and go happily to sleep, always making sure she was back on the shelf before the old lady rose in the morning.

As Christmas drew near, the old lady bubbled with ideas for the shop's window. She finally decided on a tree adorned with all of her most cherished toys. A tree was ordered, and when it arrived, the old lady set to work, decorating it branch by branch till it was almost finished. All that was needed was the toy that would sit at the top.

There she placed a beautiful doll with rosy cheeks, sparkling black eyes and a cape that shimmered like spun gold.

"When I was a girl," the old lady told Moon, "it was said that the toy that stood at the top of the tree watched over all the other toys, making sure they went to the ones who would love them best."

Moon wagged his tail and, while the old lady was lighting the Christmas candles, he hid Star among the branches. He knew that Star would be his, since no one could love the little porcelain cat more.

The tree in the shop window attracted so many customers that by late afternoon on Christmas Eve nearly all the toys had been sold. The old lady was preparing to close when a huge automobile rolled up. A richly dressed woman stepped out and entered the shop. She strode around, viewing the remaining toys with disdain.

"No, no, no," she said, and was turning to leave when she spotted Star nestled in the tree's boughs. "That little cat is exactly what I'm looking for," she cried. "I must have it!"

Moon began barking frantically.

"What an annoying animal," snorted the woman. "Remove it at once!"

"He's usually so friendly," said the old lady as she dragged Moon to the storeroom and shut him in. "I don't know what's got into him."

Then she put the little porcelain cat in a box, tied it with a ribbon, and gave it to the woman.

The moment Moon was freed he rushed out to the street, but the automobile was gone. With his nose to the ground, Moon followed the scent. He followed it for hours till, far out in the countryside, he came to a long driveway at the end of which stood a magnificent house. Cautiously he crept up and looked through a window into a lighted room. There he saw an enormous Christmas tree, the woman, and a little boy.

The boy sat surrounded by a jumble of opened boxes, all of which contained various articles of clothing. The look of disappointment on his face made Moon feel very sad.

The woman also saw the boy's unhappiness and, with a hearty "Merry Christmas," gave him the box from the toyshop. Eagerly the boy tore off the ribbon and opened the lid. His face beamed with happiness as he lifted the little porcelain cat into the light.

Moon suddenly felt very selfish for wanting to keep Star all to himself. Maybe she was meant for the little boy.

Moon turned to go. He paused to take one last look back. The little boy's smile of delight was gone, replaced by a puzzled frown as he turned the cat over and over.

"But what does it do?" he asked. "Bob its head? Swish its tail? Meow?"

"It does absolutely nothing," replied the woman. "I bought it just because it was pretty."

At this the boy's frown became an angry glare. Moon watched in horror as he hurled Star against a wall, smashing the cat into pieces.

Tears poured from Moon's eyes as a maid swept the pieces into the box and carried them from the room. He raced around to the rear of the house and waited. Soon the maid appeared and tossed the box onto a rubbish heap. Rushing forward, Moon nosed off the lid. He let out a howl of grief at the sight of the shattered remains of his friend.

Heartbroken, Moon replaced the lid and, carefully holding the box in his jaws, began the long journey home. The snow, which had been falling gently, now turned into a blizzard. Freezing winds and gusts of snow battered him till he was so tired that he could walk no farther. Moon curled himself around the box and fell asleep.

As he slept, the storm ended and the sky cleared. Stars twinkled above as a wondrous silence filled the night, a silence broken only by the soft footfall of someone approaching.

A beautiful woman with rosy cheeks, sparkling black eyes and a cape that shimmered like spun gold came toward him. Without disturbing Moon, she brushed the snow from the box and looked in. Gently she gathered the pieces of the broken cat into her hands and held them to her heart. For a moment all the stars in the night sky seemed to blaze. Then she returned the pieces to the box, replaced the lid and continued on her way.

Moon woke to the sound of bells. It was Christmas morning. He shook off the snow, picked up the box, and resumed his journey back to the toyshop. When he finally came to the door, the old lady was overjoyed. She started to put her arms around him, but the sorrow in his eyes stopped her.

Moon walked slowly to his mat by the stove, put down the box, and curled himself around it.

"What do you have there?" the old lady asked softly, and lifted the lid.

"Bless me," she cried in surprise, "she looks just like that little porcelain cat!"

In the box was a real live kitten with a star-shaped mark on her face. Moon sniffed the kitten and barked for joy. His precious Star was whole again.

Together they lived happily in the toyshop.
As the years went by Star had kittens of her own,
all with shining stars on their faces. Each night,
when Moon and Star went to sleep, the kittens
would come and curl themselves around the pair
till, in the silvery light, they looked as if they
were cradled by all the stars in heaven.